RUDOLPH'S
LESSONS FOR LIFE

by Joie Scott-Poster and Ted Kay
based on the original story by Robert L. May

*Sometimes the
best gifts,
goodness knows,
can't be wrapped
up in ribbons
and bows.*

Illustrated by Keith Peterson

APPLEWOOD BOOKS
Bedford, Massachusetts
1996

For information please write to:
Applewood Books, Box 365, Bedford, MA 01730.

ISBN 1-55709-475-6

FIRST EDITION

10 9 8 7 6 5 4 3 2 1

Printed and bound in Singapore

There's a story we know well about one foggy Christmas night...

when a very special reindeer led a history making flight.

It's a story that's been told a million, zillion times or more,

but you've never heard it told quite like this before.

There's a lot more to that famous tale that we're about to share,

through the memories of someone who was actually there!

So, let's welcome old Saint Nick himself, we're honored that he came here,

to tell us what we never knew...about Rudolph the Red-Nosed Reindeer.

Ho-Ho-Ho! The pleasure is truly mine.
I brought something special - a gift of a different kind.
Not one that would fit in my big toy-filled sack,
no, this kind of gift is much bigger than that.

Sometimes the best gifts, goodness knows,
can't be wrapped up in ribbons and bows.
What I have for you is truly a treasure,
to keep in your heart forever and ever.

You see, the story of Rudolph, from my point of view,
isn't just about a reindeer, it's about me and you.

So, let's start at the beginning... the day of Rudolph's birth.
The doctor looked surprised, so did the nurse.
Rudolph's mother knew everything was right,
when the doctor cried, "Wow, he shines like a spotlight."

Cute little deer opened his eyes,
looked in the mirror and gasped in surprise,
"How come my nose is so big, red and shiny?
When everyone else's is brown and quite tiny?"

Rudolph's mom assured him, "We love you in every way.
You have something special that will make you proud some day."
Rudolph sighed, "Some day," but his nose still displeased him.
When he grew and started school, the reindeer there all teased him.

"Nah-nah-na-nah-nah," they called poor Rudolph names,
laughed at him and left him out of all their deerball games.
Those reindeer could have shown more consideration,
think how you would have felt in Rudolph's situation.

With it all, Rudolph was quite the considerate kind,
always trying to keep the feelings of others in mind.

CONSIDERATION

But let's not think of Rudolph as totally friendless.
He did have a few whose devotion was endless.
Friends who were there to help Rudolph pull through,
whenever his red nose would make him feel blue.

But on this day before Christmas, Rudolph was quite excited.
He was trimming the tree and using his bright nose to light it.
He knew he'd been good - no reason to worry,
as he skipped off to bed hoping morning would hurry.

While at the North Pole, my place was in a panic
as a dark fog rolled in from the Pacific to the Atlantic.
"Yo, Santa!" called a worried elf, "Check out this fog!
It's thicker than pea soup and heavy as a log!"

I wondered just how I'd see my way through it.
In a fog this thick, I'd be lost before I knew it.
I thought how the children's faith could be shaken,
finding no presents when they awakened.

So, if the fog slowed me down… I'd just have to fly faster,
go around any danger and over disaster.
Seems Rudolph wasn't the only one
with obstacles to overcome!

And when faced with a challenge, I always say,
where there's a will… you will find a way.

So, the going was slow through the dark, murky skies,
with no time to stop for a burger and fries.
The reindeer were nervous and started to whimper,
"Hey, wouldn't overnight mail have been a lot simpler?"

Even with my trusty radar screen beside me,
I still made a wish for just one star to guide me.
And that's when it happened... what a surprise!
An unmistakable light met my eyes.

It was under the tree tops, somewhere below,
the closer I got the brighter the glow.
A bedroom window was lit up and beaming,
while someone in the bedroom lay snoring and dreaming.

Just then I heard snickering from reindeer in the herd...

"Must be where Rudolph lives," they sneered, "Rudolph the Red-Nosed nerd!"

I was shocked at my reindeer for being so cruel,

and made them all promise to obey the Golden Rule.

DO UNTO OTHERS AS YOU WOULD HAVE THEM DO UNTO YOU.

Rudolph was awakened from all of the chatter,
and came running out to see what was the matter.
I told Rudolph all about our delay...
the fog and dark clouds and losing our way.

And as I spoke his shiny nose started blinking,
brighter and brighter - glowing and twinkling,
Until he cried out... "I'll save Christmas Day!
With my bright, spotlight nose, I'll light up the way."

I jumped for joy and giggled with glee,
telling Rudolph he was bound for history!
So Rudolph wrote a note to his folks in a hurry...
"Dear Mom and Dad, I'm helping Santa, don't worry."

Well, the pride Rudolph felt was more than I can say,
as he pranced to his place at the head of my sleigh.
Rudolph felt so good inside he lit up like a beam.
You could see he liked himself - he glowed with "Self-esteem."

SELF-ESTEEM

Self-esteem, as Rudolph learned, depends on no one else.
It's a matter of pride - and how you feel about yourself.

Now the other reindeer thought the whole idea was absurd.

"Rudolph leading the sleigh," they balked, "Silliest thing we've ever heard!!"

But seeing my disappointment, the reindeer changed their mood,

and turned to Rudolph cheering... "Go for it, Dude!"

From that moment on, as you might well guess,

Rudolph's idea was a shining success.

As we flew past the houses or streets with a sign on them,

we could see clearly because Rudolph would shine on 'em.

We zipped through the fog with the greatest of ease,

working together... the job was a breeze.

And before I knew it - not one gift was left.

That's what I call teamwork at its best.

We were headed back home in no time at all,

laughing and singing and having a ball.

Being part of a team sure makes everyone strong.

Makes each person feel like they really belong.

Why, I bet there's a million reasons out there,

that make "Teamwork" a very good thing to share.

The next morning at sunrise in Rudolph's home town,
the reindeer found the message that he had written down.
Everyone gathered by the town square hall,
to welcome the most famous reindeer of all.

Soon the glistening sleigh came into view,
with Rudolph still leading, downward we flew.
Prouder than proud, Rudolph came to a landing,
right where the reindeer who teased him were standing.

YOU'RE SPECIAL!

Greeted by banners, high-fives and cheers,

now Rudolph's nose brought him respect from his peers.

For Rudolph… Life couldn't be any sweeter.

He was now a hero… a bright shining leader!

OUD of YOU

NG SUCCESS

And as you've just seen, a leader can be,
someone like Rudolph or you and me.
You don't have to be famous or big or strong,
for others to want to follow along.

Come to think of it - I'd have to say,
leaders like Rudolph are born every day.
The only problem is... sometimes they don't know it,
until they're given a chance to really show it.

LEADERSHIP

So the ones who made fun of Rudolph apologized.
From this day on, he would be just one of the guys.
There were some important lessons learned that day -
about how we're all special in our own special way.

And that no matter what, we should never forget,
each creature on earth deserves our respect.
I announced that Rudolph, so special and clever,
would guide my sleigh forever and ever.

Rudolph blushed from his head to his toes,

until his fur was as red as his bright, shiny nose.

With a roar of applause, the crown began to screech…

"Ru-dolph! Ru-dolph! we want a speech!"

Rudolph held his antlers high and puffed his chest out proud.

His nose glowed bright as ever as he addressed the gathering crowd,

"A-hem," Rudolph's little voice squeaked, "I'd just like to say…

This has been a wondrous night and day."

"It's clear", he said, "that we're just like the snowflakes that fall,
We're each a little different, yet there's beauty to us all.
And standing here before you, it's my heart that truly glows,
'Cause my friends have learned to love me and I've learned to love my nose!"

Now I think Rudolph's story is the best one by far,
about respecting and accepting others just the way they are.
And when you're kind to others, the goodness in you shows,
because your heart will feel a glow as bright as Rudolph's nose.

There's a word for that, it starts with the letter "D."
A word to always keep in mind - the word is "Diversity."
It means that we're all different, from our heads to our toes,
from the clothes we wear... to the shape of our nose.

Oh, but deep inside, we're really quite alike,
we all feel great when things are good, and sad when things aren't right.
Just think how much kinder this old world would be,
with a better understanding of the word "Diversity."

Well, that's the real story - and every word is true.
I can't think of a better gift for me to give to you...
than sharing what I've learned from our little red-nosed friend.
Though this story's almost over - its lessons have no end.

Rudolph helped me understand how others feel inside,
and how we all can shine when we feel a sense of pride.
He taught me about teamwork and showing respect -
and how a leader can be the very one you least expect.

He set a fine example, courageously good -
of overcoming obstacles he never thought he could.
I've learned that heroes are lots of different things,
not just slam-dunk stars or football kings.

I'm so grateful to Rudolph for opening up my eyes,
to not judging others by their race, face or size.
So I pass this story on with hopes it will be told more,
'cause learning is one thing that we're never too old for.

Since this story is a gift, it's time to wrap it up.
Take these lessons to heart - and that is thanks enough.
And just to end this story with a bit of a different slant,
I have a wish for you that I would like to grant!

My wish is that you recognize the specialness in you,
as well as all the things that make others special too.
And so, from all of us... to those reading and listening,
may your holiday season be bright and glistening!

Rudolph's Lessons for Life